A First Flight® Level One Reader

Then and Now

By
Richard Thompson

Illustrated by
Barbara Hartmann

Fitzhenry & Whiteside • Toronto

All inquiries should be addressed to
Fitzhenry & Whiteside Limited,
195 Allstate Parkway, Markham, Ontario, L3R 4T8.
(e-mail: godwit@fitzhenry.ca)

First published in the United States in 1999.

Fitzhenry & Whiteside acknowledges with thanks the support of the
Government of Canada through its Book Publishing Industry
Development Program in the publication of this title.

Printed in Hong Kong.
Design by Wycliffe Smith Design.

10 9 8 7 6 5 4 3 2 1

Canadian Cataloguing in Publication Data

Thompson, Richard, 1951-
Then and now

(A first flight level one reader)
ISBN 1-55041-510-7 (bound)   ISBN 1-55041-508-5 (pbk.)

I. Hartmann, Barbara, 1950-   . II. Title III. Series.

PS8589.H53T43 1999   jC813'.54   C98-932956-9
PZ7.T46Th 1999

To Ruth Ann
— then she was my teacher,
now she is my friend
— Richard Thompson

Then and Now
*is dedicated to my parents,
Anne M. and Robert E. Hartmann.
Thanks for the art classes.*

— Barbara Hartmann

Then
and Now

This is a book about
Then and Now.

Then was a calf,
Now is a cow.

Then was a seed,

Now is a flower.

Then was a stone,

Now is a tower.

Then it was Spring,

Now it is Fall.

Then it was short,

Now it is tall.

Then it was round,

Now just a sliver.

Then was too hot,

Now is to shiver.

Then was an apple,

Now is a pie.

Then was an egg,

Now it can fly.

Then was "Hello!"

Now is "Good-bye..."

Then was "I can't!"

Now is "I'll try..."

Then it was cream,

Now it is butter.

Then it could crawl,

Now it can flutter.

Then was the river,

Now is the sea.

Then was a sapling,

Now is a tree.

Then was the storm,

Now it has passed.

Then was the first,

Now is the last.

Then there were many,

Now there is one.

Then it was scary,

Now it is fun.